A Cat Like That

Wendy Wahman

Henry Holt and Company
NEW YORK

Henry Holt and Company, LLC
Publishers since 1866
175 Fifth Avenue
New York, New York 10010
www.HenryHoltKids.com

Henry Holt® is a registered trademark of Henry Holt and Company, LLC.
Copyright © 2011 by Wendy Wahman
All rights reserved.
Distributed in Canada by H. B. Fenn and Company Ltd.

Library of Congress Cataloging-in-Publication Data
Wahman, Wendy.
A cat like that / Wendy Wahman. — 1st ed.
p. cm.
Summary: A cat presents the characteristics of a perfect human friend.
ISBN 978-0-8050-8942-4
[1. Cats—Fiction. 2. Friendship—Fiction. 3. Humorous stories.] I. Title.
PZ7.W1269Cat 2011 [E]—dc22 2010026952

First Edition—2011 / Designed by April Ward
The artwork for this book was done in Photoshop using the lasso tool.
Printed in March 2011 in China by South China Printing Co. Ltd.,
Dongguan City, Guangdong Province, on acid-free paper. ∞

1 3 5 7 9 10 8 6 4 2

To Olif,
a small black god
with a tremendous intellect,
a powerful hunger,
and a crumpled little tail

If I could pick a best friend in the whole wide world,

I'd pick a friend who
played all the right games,
with all the best toys,
like a paper bag
and catnip mouse,
Ping-Pong balls
and a twirly bird.

My friend would stroke me gently head to tail, but not **too** much,

and rub
under my chin
and behind my ears and—

Ooh aaah!

the base of my tail. Right there!

I'd pick a friend who would
resist tickling my tummy...

or dropping
me to see if
I land on
my feet.

(I might not.)

I'd pick a friend who
wouldn't drag me around—
I'm not a cat like that!

My friend would
let me hide in
my secret place.

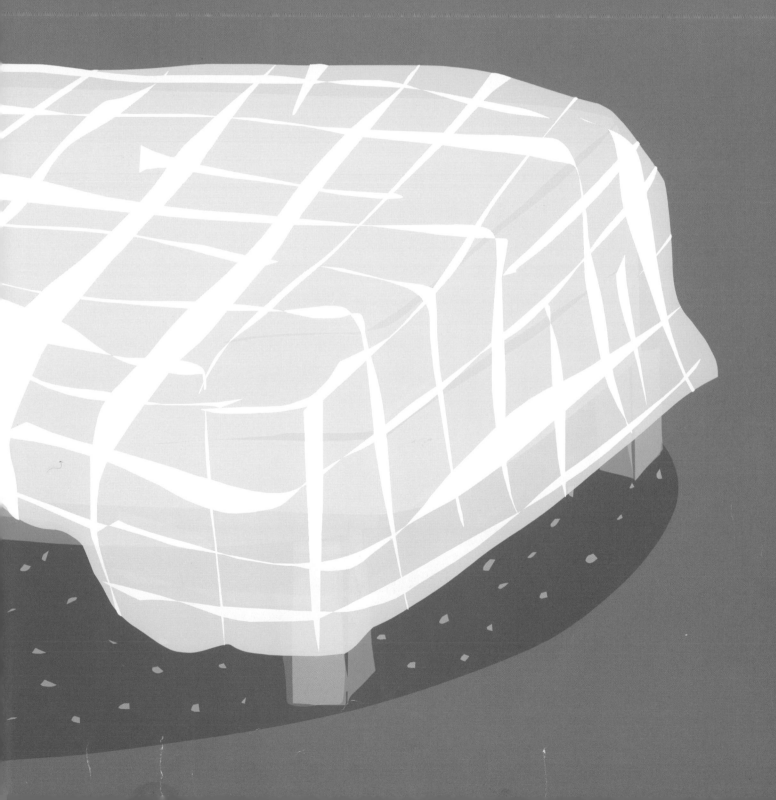

I'd pick a friend who'd
let me bask in the sun . . .

and dine in peace...

...a friend who would admire my pointy claws from afar.

My friend
would give
me privacy...

and not interrupt
my daily bath.

I'd pick a friend who can read my tail:

Happy!

I'd pick a friend
by rubbing
and purring.

I'd send a kiss with my eyes
by blinking slowly...

and hope I got one back.